# Getting from Here to There

Anne Flounders

RED CHAIR PRESS

Please visit our website at **www.redchairpress.com**.
Find a free catalog of all our high-quality products for young readers.

*Getting from Here to There*

**Publisher's Cataloging-In-Publication Data**
(Prepared by The Donohue Group, Inc.)

Flounders, Anne.

Getting from here to there / Anne Flounders.
p. : ill., maps ; cm. -- (Our green Earth)
Summary: Learn about the different ways in which people move from one place to another,
how transportation affects our air, land, and water, and how you can get there in a way that
makes a positive difference for the Earth. Includes step-by-step ideas for taking action, different
points of view, an up-close look at relevant careers, and more.
Includes bibliographical references and index.
ISBN: 978-1-939656-42-1 (lib. binding/hardcover)
ISBN: 978-1-939656-30-8 (pbk.)
ISBN: 978-1-939656-49-0 (eBook)
1. Transportation--Environmental aspects--Juvenile literature. 2. Transportation--Energy
conservation--Juvenile literature. 3. Transportation--Environmental aspects. 4. Transportation--
Energy conservation. I. Title.
HE152 .F56 2014

388                                     2013937161

Photo credits: Cover, title page, p. 4, 5, 7, 11, 13, 15, 16, 21, 23, 25, back cover: Shutterstock; TOC,
p. 8, 9, 10, 12, 17, 20, 22, 24, 26, 27, 31: Dreamstime; p. 19: Emily Bowe; p. 25: Micah Taylor; p. 27,
29: Richard Hutchings; p. 28: America Walks; p.32: © Hildi Todrin, Crane Song Photography

This series first published by:
Red Chair Press LLC          PO Box 333          South Egremont, MA 01258-0333

Printed in the United States of America

1 2 3 4 5 18 17 16 15 14

MIX
Paper from
responsible sources
FSC    FSC® C002589
www.fsc.org

# Table of Contents

# CHAPTER ONE

# Going, Going, Green!

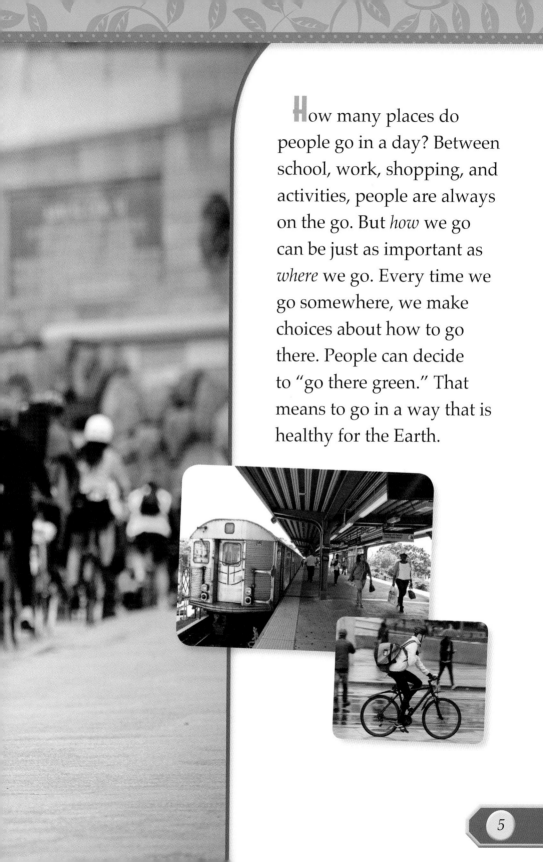

How many places do people go in a day? Between school, work, shopping, and activities, people are always on the go. But *how* we go can be just as important as *where* we go. Every time we go somewhere, we make choices about how to go there. People can decide to "go there green." That means to go in a way that is healthy for the Earth.

Transportation is how people or things move from one place to another. There are many different kinds of transportation. Cars and trucks. Buses and trains. Boats and airplanes. Bicycles and our own feet. Those are just some of the forms of transportation people use to get from here to there.

Those forms of transportation need ways to bring people from place to place. Cars, trucks, and buses need roads and highways. Trains need railroads. Boats need waterways. Airplanes need air routes. Bikes and feet need safe paths and sidewalks. These are all part of our nation's transportation system.

All over America, roads and railways run through the land. Sidewalks and roads are as much a part of our cities, suburbs, and rural areas as grass, trees, and sky. Boats sail through our lakes, rivers, and coastlines. They share the waters with marine birds, fish, and plants.

Transportation is a key part of our environment. Our transportation choices directly affect how clean our air, land, and water are. Let's find out how.

**DID YOU KNOW?**
The U.S. transportation system includes 3.9 million miles of public roads.

Source:
NationalAtlas.gov

# INTERSTATE HIGHWAY SYSTEM

The United States has a network of roadways that connects all 48 states in the continental U.S. The Interstate Highway System has a more formal name called the Dwight D. Eisenhower National System of Interstate and Defense Highways. The network is named for President Eisenhower who helped get the highways funded by the U.S. Congress in 1956. By the end of 2010, the interstate system had over 47,180 miles (over 75,930 km).

As one part of the national highway system of the U.S., Interstate Highways help military troops move between bases and airports easily. And these large highways are used to help people move out of the way of hurricanes and other natural disasters.

Although they are not connected to the system in the continental U.S., the Interstate Highway System is also found in Hawaii, Alaska, and Puerto Rico. Other highways and roads in the U.S. may be built by individual states or even local communities. While these are part of the national highway system, the Interstate system is the main group of highways with the same building standards across the entire country.

## Interstate Highway Facts

- Longest East-West: Interstate 90 from Seattle, WA to Boston, MA at 3,020.5 miles

- Longest North-South: Interstate 95 from Canadian border near Houlton, ME to Miami, FL at 1,920 miles

- Highest Point: Interstate 70 in Eisenhower Tunnel in Colorado at 11,158 feet

- Lowest Point: Interstate 8 at New River in Seely, CA at -52 feet

# On the Go

We are on the go! There are 250 million cars and trucks on the road today in the United States. Each year, those cars and trucks cover about three trillion miles. That's about the same as circling the Earth 125 million times!

**Cars get us where we need to go.**

Today, most people use cars to get where they're going. Whether it's a weekend trip or a quick visit to the grocery store, cars take us where we want to go. The average American takes about nine or 10 car trips every day. The daily trips cover about 37 miles.

## Fuel Use

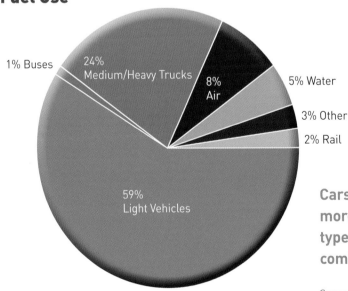

1% Buses

24% Medium/Heavy Trucks

8% Air

5% Water

3% Other

2% Rail

59% Light Vehicles

**Cars, or light vehicles, use more fuel than all other types of transportation combined.**

Source: U.S. Department of Energy, *Transportation Energy Data Book*

During a typical car trip, a few things happen that matter to Earth's health. Think about a common trip. A person drives a car two miles from home to a fast-food shop. He waits in the drive-through line to place an order. While he waits, he spends about five minutes **idling,** or running the car while it is not driving anywhere. He inches up to the window to pick up his food. Then he drives two miles home.

What happens in that single trip? First, the car burns fuel in its gas tank. Cars need to burn fuel to go. When a car burns fuel, it puts **greenhouse gases** into the air. That pollutes the air. Greenhouse gases also trap heat in the Earth's atmosphere, like a greenhouse. That makes the Earth warmer and contributes to climate change. The gases a car puts into the air are called a car's **emissions**.

When a car is idling, its engine is still running. It is still adding greenhouse gases into the air. The car also contributes to traffic on the road. If there is too much traffic, cars spend even more time idling.

Since 2010, there are now over 1 billion cars on roads around the world.

# Fueling the Way

Most cars need oil and gas to run. In the United States, we use 6,300 gallons of oil every second. Oil fuels 95 percent of our transportation. Just under half of that oil is used to fuel people's cars.

Oil is a fossil fuel. When we run out of oil, it is gone forever. People are planning now for a future in which we do not need to depend as much on oil.

Driving our cars adds more to air pollution and climate change than any other human activity. So what can we do? One idea is for people to use more public transportation. For example, people might take a bus instead of a car. There are many other choices about transportation that will help keep our air cleaner and our Earth greener.

## How Oil Is Used

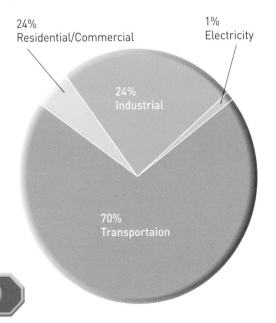

24%
Residential/Commercial

1%
Electricity

24%
Industrial

70%
Transportaion

**More than twice as much oil is used to power transportation in the U.S. than all other energy uses.**

Source: Energy Information Administration (2012 data)

# FACE OFF: Riding the Rails

**Train travel can be a green transportation choice. But the United States has limited train service.**

*"I think we should have more rail service. If more people could take trains, they would not drive as much. We would burn fewer fossil fuels."*

The United States government currently runs a passenger rail service called Amtrak. Amtrak covers long distances. It does not connect the whole country. High-speed rail service, which takes people quickly over long distances, is popular in other parts of the world, such as Europe and Japan. But in the United States, we only have one high-speed route. That is the Amtrak route between Boston and Washington, D.C. In 2009, President Obama proposed more high-speed rail in the U.S.

*"The United States is a big country. I don't think we could ever connect it all by rail. It would be too expensive. Amtrak already loses money! I think we should invest more in electric cars. They are clean. And we already have roads."*

It's true that Amtrak has lost money overall. But the high-speed route between Boston and Washington, D.C. has made a **profit** for Amtrak. Still, many are concerned that investing more money in rail service will cause the country to lose money. No one is quite sure how many people would use the service. And the United States is more spread out than Japan and countries in Europe where high-speed rail is popular. Those places have less land and more people living closer together.

**What do you think?**

# CHAPTER TWO

# Cars and Drivers

**B**uying a new car can be exciting. People look at the car's style and its features. They sit in it to make sure it's the right fit for themselves, their families, and other passengers. But another important feature to think about is how Earth-friendly a car might be. How much fuel does it burn? How much does it contribute to air pollution and climate change?

Getting more miles per gallon of fuel is good for Earth and saves the driver money, too.

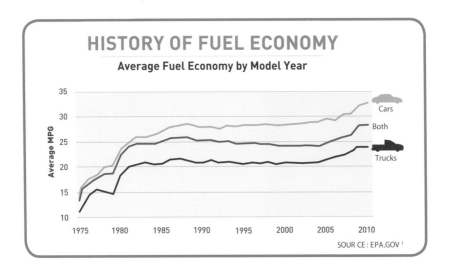

**HISTORY OF FUEL ECONOMY**

Average Fuel Economy by Model Year

Cars

Both

Trucks

SOUR CE : EPA.GOV [1]

Each gallon of gas that a car uses puts 20 pounds of greenhouse gases into the air. Some cars are built to use less gas than other cars.

Car A will travel 35 miles on one gallon of gas. Car B goes only 20 miles per gallon. Which one is better for the Earth? Car A can go farther on less gas. It puts less pollution into the air.

Cars built today use less gas than cars of the past. In the 1970s, foreign oil prices caused people to become concerned about using gasoline. In 1975, the U.S. Congress passed a fuel economy law. The law said that cars needed to run on at least 27.5 miles per gallon. But the law was only for cars, not for vehicles considered "light trucks."

**DID YOU KNOW?**

Every day, the average American uses more oil than water.

## Natural Gas for Cars

Most people agree that an alternative to gasoline is needed to run vehicles. One option that some are considering is natural gas. Natural gas is a fossil fuel. It still emits greenhouse gases when burned. However, its emissions are much less than the gasoline used to power most vehicles today. Natural gas can be used in a compressed form (CNG, or compressed natural gas) or a liquid form (LNG, or liquefied natural gas). It is less expensive than gasoline.

CNG has no odor and no chance of spills.

However, it does have some drawbacks. Vehicles running on natural gas tend to have lower fuel economy. The fuel tanks take up a lot of space in a vehicle. Natural gas vehicles are not widely available yet as there are not many places to buy the fuel.

Most people drove cars at that time. By 2002, light trucks, including sport-utility vehicles, were the top-selling personal vehicle in the U.S. These vehicles often run on significantly fewer than 27.5 miles per gallon of gasoline.

In 2012, President Barack Obama set new goals for the United States automobile industry. Our cars and trucks will get an average of about 36 miles per gallon by 2016. And by 2025, the average will increase to over 54 miles per gallon. When that happens, people will save money on gas. It is also good news for Earth. It will help keep our air cleaner and Earth healthier.

## Less Gas, More Green

Some cars are stars when it comes to keeping Earth green! **Hybrid** cars use two motors. One is powered by gas. One is electric. The car senses when it is best to use either the gas engine or the electric motor. That lets the car use gas only when it really needs to. Cars with hybrid systems use less gas than cars that run only on gas.

Hybrid cars shut down their engines when the car idles. That helps keep the air clean. When a car stops for a red light or sits in a traffic jam, the gas engine shuts down. This happens automatically. The engine stops burning gasoline. The car stops putting greenhouse gases into the air. When the driver presses the gas pedal, the engine starts again. This system is also finding its way into non-hybrid cars.

Hybrid engines can switch from gas to electric battery power.

Some cars need no gas at all! Electric cars run on battery power. People who own electric cars can drive about 60 to 120 miles on the battery. Then they need to plug in the car to charge the battery. Electric vehicles do not emit any greenhouse gases.

Driving fewer miles is an important way to help Earth. That is true no matter what kind of car a person drives. If one person drove just one fewer mile each day, it would be as if we took 240 cars off the roads for a year.[1]

Electric cars can be charged at home or at charging stations.

## How can drivers go fewer miles?

**Combine trips.** Rather than going out once to the store and a second time to the library, go out once and hit both.

**Map the trip.** Drivers who need to go to the bank, the drugstore, and the post office can choose locations that are close to one another.

**Share the ride.** Drivers may carpool if they are going to the same place.

**Walk or bike.** If the trip is short and the route is safe, consider foot or pedal power.

[1] Source: University of Maryland

## Walkable Communities

Some communities are walkable communities. That means that they are designed so that people do not have to drive very often. Each neighborhood has a center, such as a main street. They have schools, homes, and businesses all in walking distance of one another. The streets and sidewalks are designed for walkers and cyclists. There are parks and places for people to get out and enjoy.

Today, New York City has been ranked as the most walkable large city in the United States.[2] Most people can run their daily errands on foot. Schools, libraries, banks, restaurants, and shops are concentrated in neighborhoods where residents can reach them by walking.

Walkable communities offer opportunities to stay healthy and fit and connected to one's neighbors.

[2] Source: Walk Score®

**Do you think you might be interested in a career that helps people move around cities more easily?**

Here are just a few of the jobs you could do.

*Architect*     *Environmental Specialist*
*City Planner*     *Transportation Engineer*

**EMILY BOWE**

Emily Bowe's interests run from architecture to environmental science to geography. But they all come together for this University of North Carolina student in her desire to work in city planning. "Without thoughtful planning, a city is limited on how it grows and how liveable it is. A liveable city is one where all people have access to the parks and recreation spaces. People can get to and from work with ease. A city also benefits with improved storefronts when more people are walking and biking," says Emily.

Parks are placed throughout the city. Public transportation is widespread. People living in just about any neighborhood in New York City do not have to go far to find a bus stop or subway to take them a longer distance.

Across the U.S., communities are exploring how they can become more walkable. Rural areas present a challenge. People and businesses are usually quite spread out. There may be no sidewalks for people to use. Planners look at different types of solutions in these areas. They might suggest wide, paved shoulders on roads and clear, safe crosswalks across busy roads.

# CHAPTER THREE

# Greener and Greenest

**A** great way to reduce traffic is to take **public transportation**. That is transportation that everybody can use together. Everyone pays a fare to ride. Buses, trains, subways, ferries, and airplanes are all types of public transportation. Every day, 14 million Americans use public transportation. That's a good green choice. Using public transportation means we use less energy. Fewer fossil fuels are burned. There are fewer cars crowding the roads.

The Staten Island Ferry makes 55 trips each day in New York City.

Trains can be a greener way to travel.

## Buses and Trains

Public transportation itself is greener than personal cars. Buses give off 80 percent less greenhouse gases than a car. Trains powered by electricity emit almost no greenhouse gases. People who use public transportation drive 4,400 fewer miles each year than people who do not.[3] The more people use public transportation, the cleaner our Earth can be.

Of course, public transportation needs to be available so people can use it! Buses need to run around the clock. Trains need to connect the places people want to go. Every big city has a public transportation system. But many towns do not.

[3] Source: Pennsylvania Department of Transportation

Or they may have a small system that does not run often enough. The good news is more people are using public transportation, and more people want to use it if it is available. So communities are looking for ways to meet that need.

Many people would like to take trains across greater distances. Today in the United States, there is very limited rail service across distances. High-speed rail is even less available. There is only one high-speed rail service, Amtrak's Acela train, which runs between Boston and Washington, D.C. This train is much slower than the high-speed rail systems that run in Europe and parts of Asia. High-speed rail offers a fast and Earth-friendly way to cover long distances. But it is slow to catch on in the U.S. Cost is one issue. Placement of rails is another. The United States is a large country. Its cities have built up around the Interstate Highway System and the use of cars. It may be difficult to connect the whole country by means of a new rail system.

Buses and trains allow riders to relax while moving around.

## Pedal Power

One of the cleanest and greenest ways to get from here to there is to ride a bike. Bikes are powered by people, not by oil and gasoline. Bicycling is great transportation for people who have bikes and safe places to ride them.

What if people don't have their own bikes? No problem! Many communities offer bike-sharing programs. People pay to join the program. They can then borrow a bike whenever they need to. Bike-sharing programs have been successful in many cities and college campuses across the country. Every year, more towns and cities create bike-sharing programs.

Cities around the world have bike-share programs like this one in Boston, Massachusetts.

**DID YOU KNOW?**

The United States is setting up a U.S. Bicycle Route System. That is a system of safe roads and routes that will connect states, cities, suburbs, and rural areas for long-distance cyclists.

People who want to use bikes as transportation need safe bike paths and lanes. These paths and lanes need to be built where people want to go. Bike lanes and paths are being built in communities across the United States. But we still have a long way to go before biking is easy for everyone.

## CYCLES ON THE GO: MINNEAPOLIS

Minneapolis, Minnesota, is pedaling into the future! It is a city where bicycling is very popular. The city supports cycling with a bike-sharing program and 100 miles of bike paths. One of those paths is the Midtown Greenway. It cuts across five miles of the city's downtown area. The path is lit at night for safety. It is plowed in the snowy Minneapolis winters. It is a fast and safe way for cyclists to get from here to there. Even the mayor uses it!

"To be able to get around on your bike gives you a connection to the place where you live that's very different than moving around in your car," says S. Scott Dibble. He is a Minnesota State Senator from Minneapolis.

# Feet on the Ground

Walking is a great, green way to get around. For those who are able, walking is healthy for the environment and healthy for the body.

One out of every four car trips in the United States is less than one mile. Should a person replace small car trips with foot power? It depends. Here are some factors to consider.

**Is there enough time?** It might take a person 15–30 minutes to walk one mile, but only a few minutes to drive.

**Is there a safe place to walk?** Sidewalks are the safest place to walk. Marked crosswalks help people cross a street safely. The route should be well-lit, well-traveled, and in good condition.

**How's the weather?** If it's raining or snowing, it may not be pleasant to walk!

**How much traffic is on the road?**
If there is a lot of car traffic, walking might be faster.

Sometimes walking or biking makes sense. If it does, try it! The Earth will thank you for keeping it clean and green.

# Plan a Walking School Bus

Try it Out

Taking a school bus to school is a green way to go. One bus full of kids emits fewer greenhouse gases than 40 cars with one or two students in each. But there's one kind of school bus that emits no greenhouse gases at all. It's a walking school bus!

In some communities, groups of kids walk to school together. They call their groups "walking school buses". Here's how you can plan one, too.

**Step 1:** Find an adult or adults who will walk with you.

**Step 2:** Invite students to join the walking school bus.

**Step 3:** On a map, plot each student's home and the school. Plot a route that starts at the house farthest away from the school. Plan stops to meet each walker along the way.

**Step 4:** Test out the route. Make sure it has safe sidewalks and crosswalks. Keep track of how much time it takes to walk.

**Step 5:** Plan your route so everyone gets to school on time. Decide how often you will walk. Daily? Once a week? Once a month?

**Step 6:** Have fun and make friends along the way!

**Name:** Yolanda Savage-Narva

**Job:** National Campaign Director, America Walks

### Can you describe your job?

**Yolanda Savage-Narva:** I see myself as a connector. I like to connect organizations to America Walks to help make their communities more walkable. I connect people in other ways, too. At the federal, state, local and tribal levels, I usually say, "Hey, guys. Walking is important. How do we incorporate that into some kind of policy where we make sure that people have what they need to walk safely where they want to go." We also help individual communities develop a walking campaign. I work through all those levels to make walking and walkability the "in" thing to do for everyone.

### What does a walkable community look like?

**YSN:** If we talk about an urban setting, a walkable community has a crosswalk so people can go from one place to the next safely; good sidewalks; aesthetics, or things that are pleasing so people will want to walk. A walkable community has a destination. In an urban community, there have to be places for people to go. It has to be part of their lifestyle and what they do. Usually urban settings are more compact, so there are destinations. People can walk to work, and on their way to work they can drop their child off at school. Or they can pick up something from the drugstore.

### How about for a rural or suburban setting?

**YSN:** It's a little bit different. In those settings, people are looking for walking paths for recreation, not transportation. So we want to make sure those places have paths that are clear, safe, and accessible. And maybe they have marker points so people can gauge how much they're walking or how long it takes them to get around a specific walking trail. Because [these communities are] more spread out, the purpose of walking is a little bit different.

## How does America Walks encourage kids to get out and walk?

**YSN:** We work closely with Safe Routes to School National Partnership. We recognize that most kids aren't walking to school today. In the 1960s, about 48 percent of kids walked or biked to school. Today, the total that walks and bikes to school is about 12 percent. AW is encouraging parents to get involved. We know there are differences in neighborhoods. For neighborhoods that have safety issues—both public safety and traffic safety—we encourage people to get out and be visible. The Walking School Bus is a very effective tool. We're also interested in launching public campaigns in neighborhoods to tell parents that there's safety in numbers. We encourage people to walk in groups and wear clothing that's visible for people to see.

## Why is walking a good way to get from here to there?

**YSN:** Walking can make the world a better place. Walking reduces the amount of air pollution we have over time. If we all get out and we give off our own carbon dioxide to the atmosphere, the trees and flowers can in turn give us more oxygen. That gives us cleaner air to breathe and a nicer environment to be in. I [also] think when people get out and walk, we get to know our neighbors and the place we live. As a result, we have more respect for our environment and our community.

**Check it out:** americawalks.org

# GLOSSARY

**emissions**     production and release of something such as gas or radiation

**greenhouse gas**     natural and man-made gas in the atmosphere that absorbs the warmth created by the sun's heating of Earth's surface; water vapor, methane, carbon dioxide ($CO_2$)

**hybrid**     something made from combining two or more different parts or features of things

**idling**     when a motor or engine runs slowly, not fully engaged in movement

**profit**     financial gain; the difference between amounts earned and spent

**public transportation**     buses, subways, and other forms of getting around that charge set fares, run on fixed routes, and are available to all people

# FOR MORE INFORMATION

## Books

Furgang, Kathy and Adam Furgang. *On the Move: Transportation.* Rosen, 2008.

Boothroyd, Jennifer. *From the Model T to Hybrid Cars: How Transportation Has Changed.* Lerner, 2011.

## Web Sites

**Traffic Safety Kids Page:** *Tips for staying safe when walking, biking, or taking public transportation.*
www.safeny.ny.gov/kids.htm

**Walk/Bike to School:** *Want to go green when going to school? This site tells you how.*
www.walkbiketoschool.org

**Walk Score:** *How walkable is your neighborhood? Find out!*
www.walkscore.com

*All web addresses (URLs) have been reviewed carefully by our editors. Web sites change, however, and we cannot guarantee that a site's future contents will continue to meet our high standards of quality and educational value.*

# INDEX

## About the Author

Anne Flounders has lots of on-the-job experience writing for kids and teens. She has written and edited magazines, nonfiction books, teachers' guides, reader's theater plays, and web content. She has also recorded narration for audio- and ebooks. Anne protects our green Earth with her husband and son in Connecticut.